# MANTRA
## *The Medium*

MARVELLOUS MANDAKINI

BLUEROSE PUBLISHERS
India | U.K.

Copyright © Marvellous Mandakini 2024

All rights reserved by author. No part of this publication may be reproduced, stored in a retrieval system or transmitted in any form or by any means, electronic, mechanical, photocopying, recording or otherwise, without the prior permission of the author. Although every precaution has been taken to verify the accuracy of the information contained herein, the publisher assume no responsibility for any errors or omissions. No liability is assumed for damages that may result from the use of information contained within.

BlueRose Publishers takes no responsibility for any damages, losses, or liabilities that may arise from the use or misuse of the information, products, or services provided in this publication.

For permissions requests or inquiries regarding this publication, please contact:

BLUEROSE PUBLISHERS
www.BlueRoseONE.com
info@bluerosepublishers.com
+91 8882 898 898
+4407342408967

ISBN: 978-93-5819-381-7

Cover design: Tahira
Typesetting: Tanya Raj Upadhyay

First Edition: February 2024

# INTRODUCTION

Some souls are born with a destiny to be connected with a parallel world. This is a rare occurrence; however, many circumstances can come together for a soul to experience it. The character in this story is Mantra, a child who was unwanted from the womb, but destiny had something to do with her birth. Mantra's father Mr. Randhir Gowda was a famous merchant who travelled most of the time. His wife Mrs Shanta Gowda, was a homemaker who was carrying a four-month baby in her womb. It was during this time Mr Gowda had to attend the funeral of his close friend. The sudden death of his young friend shocked him, he felt heavy as he walked home after the funeral. As a tradition, he was not supposed to attend any funerals when there was a pregnant woman at home. A belief people in the small village of Sadashiva followed.

When Mr. Randhir reached home, Indira, the mother of Mrs. Shanta looked tensed seeing her son-in-law, she was a spiritual old lady who could sense entities from parallel worlds. Someone invisible from the graveyard had accompanied Randhir. Shanta felt uncomfortable that evening. She was behaving strangely. The thought that she was going to give birth to another girl child disturbed her. Being a mother of four girls, a demand for a son kept her worried. A few days later, Shanta rushed to the hospital to drop off the unborn child. Mr. Someshwar Gowda got a call from the hospital that his daughter-in-law wanted to drop her child, which could be a risk for both the child and the mother. The entire Gowda family was rushed to the hospital. Living in a joint family, Shanta was an obedient daughter-in-law, but why did she make this decision to drop her child, she had an answer, she felt that giving birth to a girl child would create a burden for the family. There was a need for a boy to take care of the estates that the family had inherited. But destiny had planned that a girl child must be born.

"A girl child again, God, have mercy on me, how will she survive in this man's world?" Shanta cried holding her daughter. An astrologer was called to forecast the life journey of the child, the first alphabet showed up as "M" according to the nakshatra, so she was named Meenakshi. As the years flew, Meenakshi grew to be bold and fearless. Her bond with her grandma Indira was very powerful, she told her stories of God and Goddess and guided her to spend time in meditation and prayers. When Meenakshi was five years old, playing with her friends, she heard the sound of bones clashing with each other, her friends asked her to sit and stand, and as Meenakshi did so the sound increased. It was amusing to them. Indira who was watching all these small shenanigans looked worried. Something was not okay.

She called Meenakshi and asked her to sit and stand again. The sound of the bones clashing was heard. Indira looked tense. 'Will this child bring home the glory of being a medium?' she was in deep thought.

Meenakshi played with her friends, she was never afraid to walk in darkness even during power cuts.

Since the age of seven, Meenakshi slept on the floor with two thick mats. She used to hear some sound beneath the floor despite there being no space or accommodation beneath it. She used to wake up suddenly at night and try to sleep again but the sound of people talking and working was a daily routine. She shared this with her mother but was ignored. When she told her grandma about it, Indira gave her a solution to chant the name of Lord Shiva. Meenakshi said Om Naamah Shivaya every day before going to bed. This chanting gave her confidence that she would not hear the sounds from the floor. Meenakshi often wondered who were the people living under the soil.

Her grandma told her stories of Gods and Goddesses. Meenakshi's inclination towards God increased as the sounds stopped when she chanted the holy names. Her grandma called her by the nickname 'Mantra' as she chanted Lord Shiva's name every night for she believed He would come to protect her as she slept.

# Table of Contents

Chapter 1:
The first encounter: Seven days of slumber ............. 1

Chapter 2:
Old Lady With Red Eyes ............................................. 9

Chapter 3:
The Man Who Grew Tall And Short ........................ 15

Chapter 4:
Learning Bicycle In Cemetery ................................. 24

Chapter 5:
The Satyanarayana Pooja ........................................ 30

Chapter 6:
One Night In The Basement. .................................... 35

Chapter 7:
Who Visits You When You are Asleep... ................ 40

Chapter 8:
The Trap Of Destiny, The First Message ................ 46

Chapter 9:
Biryani And Wine For The Jogging Soul ................ 50

# CHAPTER 1:

# The first encounter: Seven days of slumber

Mantra had summer holidays; she loved to play. She was too talkative and had many friends. Her mother found it difficult to stop her from going out. It was a bright, sunny day. Her mother had planned to send her to her aunt's place. It was a 5-kilometre walk to deliver a parcel. Mantra loved to visit her aunt, as there she could get raw mangoes to eat.

'Now listen, mantra; here is a road map; I'm telling you how to get to your aunt's place, her mother said.

'Why? Are you not coming with me, Maa?' Mantra asked.

'No, I have to prepare lunch; today is Saturday. We have guests at home', the mother said. 'How do I get there? I may miss my way'

'I will guide you; listen carefully. First comes the home of the King and the Queen; you need to take the straight road. You will see a huge wall. There may be a fire on your left side; you may see it burning. Adjacent to it, there is a mud road. Take the mud road, keep walking straight, and don't turn anywhere until you see a tar road. Cross the road; on your right side, you will see many stone slabs on a playground. Don't walk inside that playground. Keep walking straight. You get a Shiv temple. Next to it is your aunt's home. Did you understand Mantra?' the mother asked.

Mantra nodded her head. She was looking for paper and a pencil to draw the road map. She tried to draw images of the places her mother had explained.

'Hurry up, girl, you better come early; don't sit playing with your friends' Shantha said. 'I will come home directly after I give this parcel, maa ', said Mantra.

Mantra thought it was better to run and walk a little to cover the distance faster. She can also get more time to play. She had her own plans to get the work done faster.

On the way to Aunt's house, Mantra thought she should play first at Shobha's house and later run to give the parcel.

'But Maa is watching me from the window. There is no way to escape. I should go straight to my aunt's place, said Mantra.

Mantra took the parcel and started to walk; her first landmark was the home of the King and Queen.

'Ha, I have reached the first place; now the straight road is here ', said Mantra. '

But something was strange, she felt. Why was the home of the King and Queen a temple? Why did it have a fence? Why did no one enter that place? All thoughts were flowing in her mind.

'God, a basket of lemons again with flowers and pink colour on it', said Mantra, looking at the corner of the road.

It was noon, and the sun was too bright for her. She was alone on the road when she heard a voice.

"You are so beautiful."

Mantra felt good. 'Yes, I'm beautiful!', she said. continued her walk. She didn't know who said it, as there was nobody on the road, but she didn't care much.

'There is my next mark, a huge wall, said Mantra. She was wondering why there was a huge wall dividing the open land. Little did she know it was a cremation ground. The fearless child walked and ran in the dusty noon with a parcel in her hand. The walk was long, and Mantra frequently looked at the paper sketch she had made. Now and then she looked around; the vehicles didn't move on the muddy road she took. She crosses the tar road. There in her right hand was a huge field with stone and marble slabs stuck upright in rows and columns. Mantra wondered what was written on those slabs. Why do people put so many slabs in a row? This was another cemetery she was passing through. Now Mantra was tired; she thought if she could keep walking, she would not get time to play. So she starts running on the silent road. All the way, she had seen only two people. Soon she will be reaching the Shiva temple. But she felt someone was there behind her. She turned twice, but nobody was there. She ignored it, as she didn't see anyone. Hearing the temple bells, Mantra felt excited. She ran through the road and went on to ask people the address of her aunt. At last, she met her aunt Devika.

Aunt Devika gave her mangoes to eat. Mantra had meals as though she had not eaten for ten days. Her aunt was surprised, as a ten-year-old doesn't eat that much food. But seeing Mantra eating, she served her food happily. Mantra played with her cousins that afternoon. The time flew by in laughter, and soon she realised she had to go home. It was about to be 4 p.m. The mantra was now tense.

She took leave from her aunt Devika and rushed home. She ran as fast as she could. On the way back home, she saw a huge fire on the ground. Some people come there. They were crying. She didn't know why they were crying when they were setting the fire. She just had to reach home.

Knowing her mother will be angry for playing, she goes to her neighbour's house. Her friend Shobha could help her enter her home, Mantra thought.

Seeing her coming, Shobha rushed out of her house. 'Where have you been since morning, Mantra? I was waiting for you.' She said.

'Please help me. I got late playing at Devika's aunt's place. Maa will be angry. Help me. Please tell her I was at your place' said Mantra.

'Oh, I got a plan; it is time for evening prayers. I will tell your mother you were with us attending the evening prayers!', said Shobha.

Mantra found that it could be a better plan. She stood for the evening prayer in their home.

Suddenly, 'I can't see; please give me some water', saying that she collapsed.

Shobha's family was tensed; all gathered to wake her, but her eyes were rolled up. Mantra could only remember her friends carrying her by her hands and legs and bringing her home. She wasn't responding.

Mantra was in a deep sleep. A message was sent to all relatives: Mantra may not be there. She was rushed to the hospital. Doctors didn't take her case as her body was not responding. She wasn't moving. She was rushed to a civil hospital. For seven days, Mantra slept. Indra, her grandmother, was called. All were praying; medicine didn't have much effect on her. Injections were given to wake her, but every day was too hard for her family to just wait for her to open her eyes. Her mother was blamed for sending a child alone at noon.

One day, Indira called a priest from her village. He visited the hospital. He took a dry lock of grass and rotated around the cot where Mantra was sleeping. He prayed for an hour; later, he said the spirit at the corner of the road liked her and spoke to her. He wanted her to be his friend; that's the reason he followed her home. Seeing her standing for prayers, he got angry and tried to harm her. But he was asked to leave by the goddess of the home, where Mantra offered the evening prayers. There was an argument between the goddess and the spirit. Now it's asking to leave. Never send her on that road for a month. Rituals were performed to keep Mantra safe. Holy prayers were chanted by the priest. After seven days, Mantra opened her eyes. She found herself in the hospital. Doctors said she should eat lots of chocolate as she needs more glucose in her body. Her grandma smiled, saying yes, we all love to give her chocolates, as she had a bad dream.

This was the first encounter with a parallel world at the age of ten. Mantra had experienced the spirit world, but she didn't know what its depth was.

# CHAPTER 2 :

## Old Lady With Red Eyes

Miss Shanta gave all her tough household work to Mantra. She thought that physically, Mantra was stronger and could do the work easily. Mantra was now in Grade 10. She was asked to carry fifty pots of water from a pond that was seven kilometres away to fill the water tank. During the summer, there was a shortage in water supply. But for Mantra, getting water was an easier task than sitting at home and cooking food for twenty-five people.

One night, there were surprise guests at home. Mantra was asked to get sugar from the neighbourhood to prepare the dessert. It was late at night, half past nine. The streets were lonely. The moonlight was soothing. Mantra walked on the roads, watching the moon. The shops that were close to their home had closed. She had to walk a little further. This was close to the home of the King and Queen. Mantra walked on the silent road. An old lady was sitting beside the road, washing the utensils. She was staring at Mantra. Seeing the shop door half open, Mantra rushed to get the sugar. But the shopkeeper was desperate to close the doors. He gave Mantra the sugar without measuring and asked her to leave as quickly as possible.

Mantra was surprised but happy that she got more sugar at a lower cost. Something was strange there. The old lady has now stopped cleaning the utensils. Mantra looked at her. The colour of the eyes of the old lady was red. First Mantra thought she must have seen wrong or assumed it. She turned back again and took a second look at the old lady. She confirmed her eyes were red. A weird look in her eyes made Mantra feel a chill around her. For a second, Mantra felt as though she had lost her control to move ahead. Again, she turned around, but the old lady with red eyes didn't blink.

'Oh my God, why did she drink alcohol? I thought only men were drunk', said Mantra.'

'It's getting cold; though it's summer, I should run home as fast as I can, but my legs are feeling too heavy; I'm unable to even walk.'

Thinking about the old lady, Mantra headed towards home. Her grandma waited for her near the gate.

'Did you see an old lady with red eyes?' Indra asked.

'Yes, I did; this neighbourhood has gone mad; I knew only men drink; an old lady I saw today also drinks.'

'See how she looked at me; like this, her eyes were staring at me without blinking. I was thinking if I should ask her if she wanted help going home; help her reach home?' The mantra described the total appearance of the old lady.

'The best part is the profit I made today, as the shopkeeper gave so much sugar at less cost,' Mantra added.

Indira looked tensed. Mantra asked if she should go back and help the old lady reach her home; if she was overdrunk, unable to balance herself to reach her home, or may fall on the road, nobody may be able to help her then, as the street was deserted. But her grandma stopped her, saying there were guests at home.

It was half past eleven now. Mantra was shivering as though it were winter. She sat with her notebook to study, with a blanket wrapped around her. Indira was watching all this in minute detail.

'Are you okay? In summer, you need a blanket', said Indra.

'I don't know why I'm feeling a mint chill around me, grandma. I'm feeling as if something has taken my sleep. I'm feeling empty inside', Mantra said.

After all the guests slept, the bedroom lights weren't off that night. Indira sat beside her granddaughter, holding her hand. Mother got late clearing the kitchen. Indira told stories of Lord Rama to Mantra. All evil will be destroyed in the name of Rama. Mantra was asked to chant the name of Rama for ten minutes. With complete devotion, Mantra closed her eyes and chanted Rama, Rama, Rama... Meanwhile, Shanta came, and Indira explained to her. Both looked tense.

I don't understand how I missed this day; at least you should have reminded me during the day; we could have avoided her going out', said Indira to Shanta.

It was the day of the spirit, an old folktale being shared in the village. An old lady with red eyes comes once a year to clean the tombs of the King and Queen. Anyone who comes across her time will be punished by her for disturbing her duty hours. All the descriptions suited that folktale. Now Mantra is shivering in the summer. They just sat beside her, taking the name of their family deity. On a sleepless night, the sound of the hounds echoed through the streets. There were sounds of anklets echoing through the night, right around the compound wall. Mantra was trying to focus on her studies, but the image of the old lady with red eyes haunted her.

The next day, Mantra was taken to the nearby temple and asked to offer alms to the poor. Prayers were chanted, and she held her head. Mantra was not allowed to go out of the house for a week.

After a week, when Mantra went to get the items for her home at the same grocery shop, she asked the shopkeeper if he knew an old lady who sat on the road a week ago. He looked surprised, saying he didn't see anyone on the road when he left after Mantra.

# CHAPTER 3:

# The Man Who Grew Tall And Short

Mantra wanted to join the defence force. She found it glamorous to work with guns and machines. Her father asked her to jog at 5 a.m. if she wanted to stay fit. But first, she had to qualify herself as a cadet by joining the National Cadet Corps to prove that she was fit to join the army. On the first day of selection, Mantra was waiting in the long queue on the college playground. By half past one, she had her height and weight qualified. A senior cadet was sorting the final list. A mantra was selected. Here she met girls who were from her locality and were also interested in joining the army. Sometimes it's good to be a talkative prankster. One attracts many friends.

Saritha was a shy girl who was watching Mantra closely. She approached Mantra hesitantly and asked, 'Will you be my friend?'

Mantra nodded her head. Both walked home, as Saritha was living in the next neighbourhood. On the way, Saritha expressed her longing for morning jogging but didn't have any companions.

This was exactly what Mantra was looking forward to. She said, 'I will come at 5 a.m.; are you ready for jogging?'

Saritha agreed. The next day, Mantra woke up early, did all the home chores assigned to her, wore shoes, and started to walk out at 4.45 a.m. The streetlights were placed every 100 metres, which was enough for her to reach Saritha's place, which was four kilometres away from her home. Mantra jogged a little and walked a little. The first day of fitness, she was excited. She arrived on time. Saritha was waiting for her. Both started to walk at 5 a.m. as they had to reach an army training centre as a landmark, which was a ten-kilometre jog. A little uphill, they had to go through a lonely street; either side had huge open grounds meant for training the commandos. Mantra stood at the entrance gate of the Infantry Golf Centre, an area measuring more than fifty acres of land. She didn't enter it, as the first stop was the Military Ganesh temple uphill. Later, they decided to enter through the back gate of the golf centre to speed walk. Since Saritha insisted on visiting the temple first, she agreed to jog to the temple first. Their shoes echoed as their exhaled breaths made a rhythm of beats. After visiting the temple, they entered the golf centre. This routine continued for a few months.

After a few months, Mantra's younger brother Sampath and his friend Swapnil also joined the morning fitness routine. These boys wanted to jog early, at 4.30 am, as they had school. It was December, the roads were foggy, and the streetlights looked like Will-o'-Wisps due to the fog. Indira asked Mantra not to jog early, but Mantra denied it, saying it's a fitness routine and it's thrilling to jog in the fog. Seeing her brother jog early, she too decided to be there early, along with Saritha.

One day, when Mantra was jogging, she saw a man near the bus stop at 4.35 a.m. He was taller than the average height of any man. The streetlight was flickering. Sampath and Swapnil were just five steps ahead of her. They were the first ones to see him. Mantra saw this man whose head reached the bus stop's roof, which was something not normal. But seeing his height, Mantra was excited to see a man taller than twelve feet. He wrapped himself in an old, muddy yellow shawl; his matted hair and scruffy beard made him look rough. He looked at the boys and stood there. Mantra saw him walking; she wanted to reach him and take a close look, but she couldn't as he walked faster, and though she was jogging, she couldn't reach his speed. Mantra entered the colony zone to pick up Saritha. This stranger was still ahead of her. He stood at the next bus stop.

Mantra and Saritha were jogging when they saw this stranger ahead of them. But this time, his height was normal for a regular man. Mantra was talking about him to Saritha. They saw the boys ahead of them, but they were running at their best speed. Suddenly, Mantra saw the man vanish. Mantra ignored him and took a turn to reach the first Ganesh temple, only to check why the boys were running instead of jogging. Seeing Sampath and Swapnil sweating heavily at the temple with their shirts off, Mantra was surprised.

'Did you see that man?' Sampath asked, 'He was a ghost, and his height increased more than the normal range.'

'Yes, God Ganesh, please save us. He looked at us as though he wanted to take us with him. I'm not going to walk or jog tomorrow', Swapnil said.

'I saw his tall height; later, he was normal. I think he knows magic to increase and decrease his height, like the one you see on television', Mantra said.

'But I don't know why you boys are sweating so much; he is only fooling you. Come, let's go for the second round of jogging.'

'Are you crazy? Do you think he knows magic?? He is a ghost. I will tell Maa not to send you out tomorrow; girls are caught first. They like girls; what if he comes with you and asks for more food? Are you going to eat more and grow tall like him?' Sampath was silent.

'Okay, you boys, stay here. Saritha and I will jog and pick you up after our routine workout.'

'I think these boys are just jealous of seeing a man taller than them. Come, let's jog.'

They started jogging again.

Mantra saw the same man, who grew tall. He was there under that streetlight. 'I think he likes streetlights' she said, and he waits on the bus stops.

'Hey, look, that man is increasing his height again. Come, let's see if he is a ghost'. Mantra said.

'Saritha, increase your speed; we should be able to reach him; God knows what height he has.'

'Yes, we can do it; we have to reach him. Come on, let's speed up a little more.'

The man walked faster than our jog. His speed was faster. Mantra wondered how a man could know so much about magic: 'Saritha, look, he decreased his height in darkness; he knows magic; come, let's run to catch him; what stamina he has got.'

They tried their best to reach him, but he always remained ahead of them, and he was only walking.

They almost reached him just when a truck passed them, and they lost him. But later in the second, they saw him again, about 500 metres ahead. There was not a soul around.

Mantra wondered how a man could have such stamina to walk so fast. 'I wish I had that speed; I could qualify in my fitness test for the army.' Again, he stood under the streetlights where the four roads met.

They kept a watch on him, and he decreased his height again to that of a normal man. Suddenly it got foggy, and by the time they reached him, he had vanished within a matter of seconds.

Mantra couldn't get him out of her mind. They reached the military Ganesh temple, offered their salutations to Lord Ganesh, and walked back to pick up the boys.

Both were pale in fear. 'We spoke about the man and how he vanished. Hearing us', Swapnil said, 'I am not going to come tomorrow'.

They reached home, seeing Sampath. Maa asked if he had had a heavy workout. Mantra told her about the man who knew magic, but Sampath cut off their conversation, saying they saw a ghost. In the evening, Papa was called by Swapnil's father; he had a fever and was restless. Sampath, too, got a high fever. The boys spoke a strange dialect in fever. Now the tension at home has increased. Grandma asked Mantra what had happened, and she simply said, 'We saw the man at the bus stop who knew magic as he knew to increase and decrease his height.'

Mantra was asked to stay at home and not step out after dusk. There was a myth that a man from the spirit world came to check on the place once a year.

He had a boundary area where he took rounds only on that track.

They had disturbed his routine by being there at that time. She didn't understand any of this, nor did she believe it was true, as according to her, he was a magician who knew how to grow tall and short. Grandma held her hand, took her to the bedroom, and asked her to describe him. Mantra narrated the entire episode. Indira was tensed.

Maa was asked not to send Mantra out for jogging. The next day, when she woke up early, she found the doors were padlocked. She was unable to go out. Sampath had a fever for two days. A ritual was done to reduce the fever. For Mantra, it was strange; she wondered how offering a wine bottle in the place where the man vanished could help his brother come out of the fever.

Mantra could tease her brother, saying he is a brave man; seeing a man taller than him, he gets a fever. After fifteen days, Mantra was permitted to jog, but only after 5.30 a.m.

# CHAPTER 4:

# Learning Bicycle In Cemetery

Mantra was eighteen years old, and she had options to either help her mother in the kitchen or help with the maintenance of the entire house, along with all the heavy work of cleaning the storage room, water tanks, and getting groceries from the market. She preferred the outdoor work. One challenge she always faced was carrying fifty kilogrammes of jowar to the flour mill. She had to walk with the help of her friend. Sometimes she was asked to make frequent runs to the shop, which was three kilometers away, to get the ingredients for the kitchen. Saturday was a day marked to clean the water tanks and all the brass utensils in the house.

On one Saturday at noon, she walks to her friend's house, just to escape the work. Suwarana was staying in a new layout that was very close to a Christian cemetery. Suwarana's father was working as an instructor in the department of physical education. He had bought a new bicycle for his daughter so that she could feel comfortable travelling longer distances.

Mantra was surprised to see Suwaran's father being so positive about nurturing his daughter, whereas in Mantra's family it was believed that girls should not ride bicycles as they would dominate the men.

'Can I also learn to bicycle?' Mantra asked.

'Yeah, you can, but what will you tell at home?' Suwarana said.

'I will manage that. Tell me where we learn. My family is huge and my relatives are everywhere. My bother has his friends who spy on me. Can you name a place where nobody can see me learning?' Mantra said.

Suwarana took Mantra to a fenced-in area. On one side, there were white, long slabs decorated with tiny button roses; on the other side, there was a huge playground. It was a rare and deserted place. Not even a bird flew there. They decided that it would be the best place to learn to bicycle. Every day Mantra rushed after her college to Suwarana's place, saying that they had combined their studies. From 5 p.m. to 6 p.m., she practiced cycling. She shared her secret learning with her best friend Vaibhavi, who was also eager to learn cycling. The three friends met in the evening, spent Saturdays and Sundays playing in the open space, rested on the white stone slabs, and walked home as though nothing had happened.

One day, Vaibhavi's mother asked Mantra where they were going every day on the hillside. Mantra said it was a combined study. Vaibhavi was very close with her mother, and she told her the truth. There was a change in the expression of

Vaibhavi's mother. She said, 'I hope nobody follows you from there; you girls better be careful.' But none of the girls understood what Aunty was hinting at.

Seeing the girls be so casual about it, her aunt said, 'It's a cemetery where you are practicing cycling. I hope you understand.'

The girls said they were sitting on the stone slabs to take turns and played the traditional four-square game. Little did they know they were sitting on coffins. Mantra thought that the cross was inserted next to the tomb in order to control the soul that has left this body. She believed that to make the departed soul happy, flowers were grown around the slab so that on the soul's day, the soul could come to meet the family members who would come to meet them.

It was evening, and as usual, the three went for their practice. Mantra was recalling what Aunty had said. She was sitting on the coffin, thinking about the person who was resting in peace beneath her. She couldn't believe it was a burial ground; it was so calm and peaceful, with no one to disturb her here.

She said, 'You people are lucky to go. Look at me, I have so much work to do: do all my homework, fill water for fifty people every day, carry heavy bags of grain, sweep and mop ten rooms, and yet Maa tells me, I'm a girl who is not behaving as a girl'.

The chill in the air didn't have any effect on her. Mantra walked home, did her regular chores, and studied. Indira watched her closely but didn't say anything. One day, Maa asked her to carry twenty kilogrammes of jowar to the flour mill. Mantra took the bag, walked a little distance up to the Mohita family, asked for a bicycle, placed the bag of jowar on the bicycle, and went to the mill. After half an hour, Mantra came back, riding the bicycle. It was a record in the Gowada family; a girl was riding a bicycle in public. Her brother screamed, calling their Maa and grandma, and all came out to see Mantra riding the bicycle at great speed with the bag of jowar tied to the carrier.

'When did you learn bicycle? Where did you learn?', Maa asked.

Mantra said, 'Just started, and it came!!' and laughed. At night, Indira held the hand of Mantra and asked her to tell about the adventure of learning the bicycle. Mantra narrated everything. Grandma was sweating; she never could even dare visit the cemetery, which was believed to be haunted, and her grandchild went every day to learn cycling there; she didn't even bathe after coming home and carried on a normal life. Indira held Mantra's hand and didn't say a word. The entire family was worried about what could happen to Mantra as she had been to the forbidden place. The following days, Mantra was told to practice bicycling in the neighbourhood; permission was granted by her father, as he felt she would be safe away from the cemetery.

# CHAPTER 5:

# The Satyanarayana Pooja

Every year, it was a tradition of the Gowada family to organise the Satyanarayana Pooja. The entire community would have a feast; it was a community event to meet people and stay connected with them all. The preparations had been going on since morning, and Mantra was busy with her cousins cleaning and setting up the furniture. The priest arrived at 4 p.m., prepared the sacred food, and chanted the names of Lord Vishnu. All stood with their hands joined to offer their salutations for the Lord. It was a feast for the community; from every household, people flocked to listen to the stories of Lord Vishnu; later, all stood for mass singing of hymns. The place vibrated with happiness and laughter. Food was served on banana leaves, and when the women were about to leave, they received gifts as a token of respect. It was time for cleaning. Mantra was getting a broom and walking towards the basement where the food had been served.

Her elder sister stopped her, saying, 'Look, grandpa is there; he is watching us. He is calling someone to help Papa'.

Mantra did see an elderly man standing there, but she didn't know whether he was their grandpa. She was recalling the face of the man standing near the staircase. She had seen him when the priest was narrating the story; he was there, sitting in the hall. When the plate of sacred rice was passed to him, he didn't take it or move. It was during this time that Mantra saw the flower garland from the photo frame fall, as though the gods themselves wanted to show their presence. She was recalling all the events that took place while the pooja was performed.

'This was not a dream', Mantra said. 'It's real'. Before she could call her Maa, the man vanished in front of her eyes. Her sister stood frozen. The distance they had to walk was not much. But at that given time, Mantra decided to run. She took a few steps backwards and said in her mind, 'On your mark, get set go...'

She ran as fast as she could. Maa was in the kitchen. There were cooks who were clearing the vessels, and the leftover food was packed to be given to the people who lived on the roadside. Mantra was breathing heavily, saying, 'There that man, sis called him grandpa'. All stood in silence. Maa denied it, saying that this was not the time to play pranks when the house was filled with relatives and guests still around. But Mantra took Maa outside and showed her sister sitting on the swing. Maa called Grandma and asked her to take care of both.

Mantra was shown the family photographs to identify Grandpa. After flipping a few pages of the family album, Mantra pointed out an elderly man with a white turban, sitting on a chair surrounded by his sons and daughters. Indira inquired twice about whether Mantra had seen the same person when the pooja was in progress. Mantra nodded. It was her grandpa, who had passed away ten years ago. That night, all the elders had a meeting about why Mantra was always facing such events in her life. One of the relatives spoke of the different ancestries one was born into, saying that as per the time Mantra was born, she belonged to the group, or what's called the "Gana" of "Manushya," while her elder sister belonged to the "Deva Gana," who could see the souls around. It also indicates that Mantra will be facing more such events in her life. Her cousins created more fearful stories about how the souls would follow her; she could sense their presence but could not avoid their movements around her. This made Mantra get tensed, as she hitherto had not known that there were souls around. She believed that the person's final departure meant that it was time to go to live with the Gods, and when the Gods opened the doors for the souls to meet the relatives, we call that day the Mahalaya or the ancestral day.

After a few days, Mantra was asking her grandma if she could change her gana to Rakshasha so that she could sleep well at night or walk without being followed. Grandma smiled, saying only Mantra is special, as she can even sense Gods who will always come to rescue her, as she was meant to help people live a life devoted to God.

# CHAPTER 6:

# One Night In The Basement.

Mantra was exploring life; she questioned all the traditions and beliefs the family followed. This led to more heated arguments with her father. Being an NCC cadet, she didn't believe whatever was told to her. One day Mantra asked to perform a ritual as she was getting angry without any reason. She refused. Her father was angry at her; he said, 'If you can't do what we are asking you to do, we will isolate you in the basement till your behaviour is corrected'. Mantra was so angry at her papa that she walked with her bedding in the basement. After the incident with her grandpa, nobody walked into the basement.

Mantra walked downstairs. Her steps echoed louder than usual. The sound of the crickets added music to the silence. The place was not cleaned for months. She took a broom that was kept in the corner of the room and swept the room. She laid the two thick, long mats on the floor, a pillow, and a blanket to wrap herself in. There was complete silence in the room, but she was not getting sleep. She tied a mosquito net above, tucked in, and tried to sleep. That night, she was restless. She felt someone was there watching her; she heard the sounds of someone breathing loudly. She thought at first the sound came from upstairs as her father snorted. Later, she heard heavy footsteps, as if someone were walking. The echo of the floor was so heavy from above that she could feel it in the basement. Sleep vanished. It must have been half past three. Mantra had closed her eyes, trying to sleep. But someone in the basement was unhappy about her presence there. The soul got restless. It blew air so hard that Mantra woke up. She could see a shadow floating above the mosquito net.

She got up, saying, 'Stop pranking me; let me see you'.

The air moved the net. There was no way the wind could move in the basement. Mantra was now alert that it was not a prank, but there was someone who was invisible. She got angry. I got up, wrapped the mosquito net, and threw it aside. The air could give her a sense that someone was taking rounds around her bedding but was unable to reach her. Mantra started to speak in an angry tone if you dare show me your presence. But now that the breaths were heavier, she could hear it louder and more clearly.

'I'm not afraid; I'm not afraid', she said.

Mantra started to chant loudly, "Om Nama Shivaya, Om Nama Shivaya, Om Nama Shivaya..."

The entity now has a heavier and more prominent presence. This went on for more than two hours. Mantra's voice was now echoing in the basement; she got louder, as loud as a loud speaker. She was sweating heavily. She could not control her anger, as the entity was not showing who he was, but he tried his best to scare Mantra and make her feel his presence. It appeared as though Mantra had gotten powers from Lord Shiva directly that night as she sat there without moving, as this soul, whoever it was, was not allowing her to move out. Mantra heard the first call of the rooster; it was forty-thirty in the morning. Still chanting Om Nama Shivaya...

'Mantra... Mantra... What happened? Come up. Why are you praying so loudly? Come up. Maa called her.

But Mantra continued to chant the name of Mahadev; she did not move. When Maa reached the basement, she was shocked to see the state of Mantra. The entire bedding was wet with sweat, and Mantra's face was sweating, but her voice was louder, asking for help. Tears flowed as she saw Maa. But she was angry that Maa had come late. She was all alone, battling with the entity; nobody knew what was happening in the basement, as all were sound asleep. Fear ran through the spine of Shanta; she held Mantra, which helped her walk the stairs. Mantra entered the prayer room and sat there for an hour. She felt her energy being drained, but she managed to walk with the support of her Maa. Her father had woken up; she threw him an angry look and went to bed.

Shanta told her husband the condition Mantra was in when she found her in the basement. He was speechless. The next day, there was no argument at home. Mantra slept throughout the day. The basement was banned for the entire family after that incident.

## CHAPTER 7:

## Who Visits You When You are Asleep...

Mantra was planning for her career, to join either the armed forces or the police department. She spent most of her time on working out and maintaining fitness after college hours. In her locality there were devotees of Goddess Renuka who would ask for alms every Friday and live a simple life. Since her family were strong believers of Goddess, Mantra too respected those forces of the universe. One day when she was coming back home after her practice with Saritha, she came across a group of ladies carrying the Goddess on their heads, they had smeared their foreheads with yellow turmeric powder. Mantra stood there waiting for them to pass by. She rushed home, as she was getting late for her college. It was a long day for her, she came home late in the evening exhausted, had an early dinner and slept.

Mantra's cot was beside a long flat swing, she had kept her books on it to study for the next day. It was late at night, all were in deep sleep. Suddenly someone patted Mantra on her hand. She opened her eyes, and she saw a lady dressed in a white saree, standing beside her cot. Smiling at her. She had a huge bindi on her forehead, dark long hair that she left loose, her eyes were bigger than the average size of any lady Mantra had come across. At first Mantra thought she was dreaming, so she slept. But there was another tap on her hand, this time the same lady was sitting on the swing. The sound of the swing woke Mantra, she sat up in her bed. The lady in white saree vanished. But the swing was still moving to and fro. Mantra stopped the swing, took her blanket wrapped herself tightly and tried to sleep.

The next day she narrated her story to her grandma, who was trying to connect the string of the events that happened. Grandma came to a conclusion that the Goddess loved her and wanted to take Mantra as her dear child. Now Mantra got tensed. She can't walk door to door asking for alms. She planned to be an officer, but didn't have any time to sit and meditate.

The following Tuesday, Mantra again had a similar experience after midnight. But this time the lady in a white saree had got a basket which was used to collect alms, she was also holding a white *chamar\** in her hand.

The next day Mantra did not say a word about the previous night's incident. She was sitting with her grandma, suddenly Mantra cried out, 'Yakunda Jogavaaa'... It was the chants the women say when they go to ask for alms

She had no control over herself, she felt a strange lightness inside her, around her she experienced a white light. Her grandma held her hand saying, 'She will not leave you until you visit her hometown'. Mantra ignores her and walks away. The next day was Wednesday, it was a day all the family members ate fish or chicken. Maa had marinated the fish and asked Mantra to fry the fish for all. Mantra loved fish fry, the smell itself made her feel hungry.

All the ladies of the home sat together for dinner. Mantra removed the bones of the fish, kept them aside and started to eat, the first bite, she felt there was hair in the fish. She took the morsel she had put in her mouth, the fish had vanished, and a thick layer of hair was there in her hand. Mantra searched the next piece of fish, it was proper roasted fish, she took a bit, again she felt it's a hair, she took the morsel she had chewed, it was again a thick matted hair in her hand. Mantra got upset. She showed it to her grandma, it was not okay, as she loved fish, now she was unable to eat it.

Indira consoled Mantra, saying, 'This was going to happen; you are not supposed to eat non-veg.' But Mantra had some other plans. The next day, she went to Vaibhavi's house and asked her to prepare chicken. She ate chicken and came home. As she reached home, Mantra started vomiting; she had a stomach upset and had severe loose motions. Now Indira had inquired about the process by which Mantra could come out of this. The solution was given to Mantra: she had to give up non-veg for six months, take a holy dip in the river Malaprabha, ask the goddess to bless her, and Mantra could donate a cow to the temple. Mantra denied following any of the solutions her grandma had suggested. The following week, Mantra sat down to cook chicken. She made the chicken curry and was preparing dosa. She sipped the chicken soup, to taste. After ten minutes, Mantra started vomiting. She was restless; she couldn't take the smell of the boiling chicken. She was forced to leave the kitchen. Later that night, Mantra decided to give up the fight to avoid health complications.

Four months had passed; now Mantra was a pure vegetarian; she was fasting on Tuesdays and Fridays; and she was spending more time in prayers, chanting the names of the goddesses. On the night Mantra was in deep sleep, she got a tap on her hand, as though someone came to wake her from her deep sleep, only to save her. She heard a voice saying, He has come to see you. Chant the name of Shiva. Mantra sat on her bed, chanting the name of Lord Shiva. She felt a chill air spinning around her; it went off as if it had come after an hour. After completing six months of devoting time to prayers and fasting, Mantra goes to the sacred hills of the Goddess, takes a dip in the holy river Malaprabha, pays salutations to the Goddess, and thanks her for protecting her. After this incident, Mantra turned out to be a pure vegetarian.

Mantra now believes in the guidance of her grandma, when we are asleep there are many things that happen in spiritual world, unknown to us.

*Chamar- Thick lock of Tibetan Yak's white hair that was used as a fan in royal settings and is also seen in hands of deities*

## CHAPTER 8:

# The Trap Of Destiny, The First Message...

The Gowda family had witnessed a series of financial losses. This disturbed the happy environment at home. Mr. Gowda went in search of answers for the downfall of his business, the answers he got were weird. There were frequent arguments at home, Mantra started to spend more time with her friends. She left the house early, came home late to avoid conversations with her father.

One day Mantra was forced to stay at home, she was restless. She was getting a weird feeling, as if something bad was going to happen, but she did not know what it was..

Her mother was a very calm lady who never scolded her children, but lately, she was getting angry. Mantra said, 'Maa don't grind your teeth, you will fall and break your bone one day'. Unknowingly Mantra had spoken the message she was hearing in her mind.

Shanta was shocked, how could her daughter speak harshly to her own mother?

After a few days, Mantra was sitting in the bedroom, Maa was busy with her work, Sampath came with a note teasing Mantra, suddenly Maa got involved in the conversation, now she started chasing him, in order to escape her, he locked the door. Before Mantra could react, Maa pulled the handle of the door, and she slipped and fell on the floor. In a fraction of a second, her wrist bone got injured.

Maa was rushed to the hospital, and on the way she recalled what Mantra had said. When Maa came back from the hospital, she asked Mantra to show her tongue, to check if she had a black mole, as it was a belief if a person who had a black mole on their tongue, whatever they spoke, could come true. Mantra was blamed for using the wrong words towards Maa. Nobody at home spoke to her. She felt helpless, now her own Maa had also turned against her. Mantra found it difficult to stay at home. She wanted to visit her grandma but was not permitted to go to the village. Months passed by. Mantra did not know how to explain what she was seeing when she was alone. The visions were like dreams with open eyes, she couldn't avoid them, nor could she explain them to anyone. Seeing the spell of unhappy events, Mr. Gowda decided to take the family for an outing. Early in the morning, the preparations were going on for a picnic. A strange pain was flowing in Mantra, she was totally silent. Unable to express what may happen to the family if they go out. She asked her Maa to avoid the outing, but her Maa denied her request.

Mantra sat outside in the courtyard washing the vessels, a thought crossed her mind, what will happen to the family if something happens to Papa...

Just then Mantra hears a loud fall. Papa slipped his feet, lost balance. His hipbone was fractured. He was rushed to the hospital; a major bone grafting surgery was conducted which costed the family a huge amount. Again, Mantra was blamed for questioning the sacred deed of going out. Her father stopped talking to her saying she was a curse to the family. Mantra was asked to stay at home and help her sisters. A series of incidents made it difficult for the family to survive, they decided to sell the house and move to their ancestorial home in the heart of the town. Mantra felt the ambiance of the house was getting worse every day. She decided to take a part-time job so that she could stay out and support her family financially. She could not see her papa bedridden. Her Maa was a helpless homemaker, she saw how big a role money played in people's behaviour. Her relatives stopped coming home. Though they had acres of land in their native, they were given respect for the huge building her papa had owned, now it was gone forever. After the marriage of her sisters, the family shifted to their ancestorial home.

## CHAPTER 9:

## Biryani And Wine For The Jogging Soul

Sometimes life takes circles and we live the same incidents again and again. Mantra kept herself busy even after shifting to her grandma's home. Mantra had to walk extra ten kilometres to reach the practice playground. She asked her Maa for a map. She guided Mantra, describing the two huge trees she had to cross, which were the landmarks. She had to keep walking straight as many small lanes joined the city areas. The first day Mantra drew the map on a blank paper and walked during the day to get a view of the place. The next day she woke up early in the morning went out jogging, came home before 7 am, helped Maa do all the household chores and rushed to work. She never spoke to her neighbours as she felt that people only come close when one has money and status. Her neighbourhood had a typical village setup, women folk woke up early, cleaned the front yards of their homes, and watered and decorated the place with rangolis. Mantra was the first to put rangoli in her lane at 5 am, the old woman in her lane wished her when she was out for jogging. Mantra carried a pair of nunchucks in her hand as she found it was safer to walk within the town which was still unknown to her. Jogging at 5 am, Mantra found it difficult to reach home before 6.30 am, she didn't want anyone to know in her locality that she was practising martial arts. She decided to go a little early and started from her place at 4.30 am.

Winter nautical dawns were more inspiring for her, she loved the beauty of the silent nature. To her surprise the men folk in that area had group walks together. They gave a silent look at Mantra when they saw her for the first day. Mantra observed the timings they all came out of their homes and did manage to leave the locality before the old men. One day she was jogging on the lonely streets, there was a huge tree that was standing as a majestic structure in the middle of the wide road. She was admiring the tree looking at its huge branches, the trunk was wrapped in a red wale, it looked as though someone gifted the tree the beauty of love. Mantra reached the tree, she heard footsteps behind her, she stopped, and the footsteps too stopped, later she heard a louder laughter of a man. Mantra did not turn back, she was so angry, she thought a man was trying to ignite fear in her seeing she is alone on the road.

'If you dare, come out let me see, don't think I will be afraid of you' Mantra said.

The voice stopped, Mantra felt someone hug her lovingly from behind, she could feel the arms of a man. For a second, she felt the deep love flowing from that unknown entity into her. The way he had held her, Mantra was frozen for a few minutes. At that moment, she felt a love so intense, that she was alert. She heard a whisper, 'You are very bold, I like your attitude'.

Mantra regained her senses and continued jogging. She could not forget the way she was held. So much love she felt in a few seconds. Later that day, as she did her office work, she was frequently getting the thought of that invisible soul. She closed her eyes and tried to meditate thinking about him. He was about thirty years old, tall and well-built. She could not see his face. She tried to focus but lost the link. Maa observed Mantra had a change in her behaviour. She asked what was disturbing her. Mantra told her about the incident that had happened. Maa rushed out to her neighbour. There was a medium in their lane who could tell them the solutions related to the spiritual world. It was the day that this soul would visit the place, the neighbourhood knew this so to make all denizens alert they had tied a red wale around the tree. This was to warn people that they should not walk out of their homes the next day to avoid any encounters. Since they were new to the place, nobody had informed them. In the evening Mantra was taken in an autorickshaw. Her father purchased biryani and a bottle of wine. Mantra was asked to touch it. The food was rotated around her along with the wine. Later it was kept near the tree. There were wine bottles at the foot of the tree, Mantra felt his presence when she reached the place. She smiled, saying that soul was very royal and that he needed biryani and wine. Her Maa asked her not to comment. Mantra was asked to stay at home for a week, her jogging was stopped. She could only leave the house at 5.30 am. Somewhere she felt that she would be talking to these souls sometime later in her life.

www.ingramcontent.com/pod-product-compliance
Lightning Source LLC
LaVergne TN
LVHW041551070526
838199LV00046B/1899